This igloo book belongs

....

igloobooks

Published in 2014
by Igloo Books Ltd
Cottage Farm
Sywell
NN6 0BJ
www.igloobooks.com

Copyright © 2014 Igloo Books Ltd

HUN001 0514
2 4 6 8 10 9 7 5 3
ISBN 978-1-78197-624-1

Illustrated by Amanda Enright

Printed and manufactured in China

What's the Time Mr Wolf?

Amanda Enright

igloobooks

"What shall I wear today?" he wonders, pulling all his clothes out of the wardrobe.

"I know, I'm going to be a Superhero!" Mr Wolf puts on his bright, red cape and sparkly super-goggles.

What's the time, Mr Wolf?

It's **8** o'clock.

Mr Wolf is hungry and his tummy is rumbling very loudly.

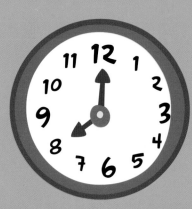

Gurgle!

What's the time, Mr Wolf?

It's **9** o'clock.

"A superhero's teeth are **always** sparkly and clean," says Mr Wolf.

Squelch!

Oops! Mr Wolf steps on the toothpaste tube. The toothpaste squirts everywhere!

What's the time, Mr Wolf?

It's 10 o'clock.

"A superhero needs a super-fast bike," thinks Mr Wolf and off he goes...

ZOOOoooom!

He waves to the three little pigs.

"Hi, little pigs!
See you
this afternoon!"
he calls.

What's the time, Mr Wolf?

It's 11 o'clock.

Mr Wolf passes by Kitty's house. Poor Kitty is stuck in the apple tree.

"**Help!**"

"Hold on, Kitty,
I'll save you!"
shouts Mr Wolf.

"A superhero
always
comes to
the rescue."

What's the time, Mr Wolf?

It's 12 o'clock.

"All this superhero work is making me super-hungry," says Mr Wolf.

"I think it's time for a little snack."

Mr Wolf buys a snack, but it's not little at all. In fact, it's enormous!

Mmmmmm!

What's the time, Mr Wolf?

It's **1** o'clock.

After a rest, Mr Wolf is feeling **Super** again.

"I think I'll go for a swim," he says.

"superheroes **always** need to keep fit."

On the diving board, Mr Wolf goes Boing! Boing! Boing! and dives in with a huge...

Splash!

What's the time, Mr Wolf?
It's **2** o'clock.

It's time for a game of football in the park.

"I'll use my **Super-strength!**" shouts Mr Wolf.

He kicks the ball really, **really** hard and scores!

GOALLL!

What's the time, Mr Wolf?

It's **3** o'clock.

Mr Wolf visits the three little pigs. They are building a new house.

Bang!
Clatter!
Bang!

What's the time, Mr Wolf?

It's **4** o'clock.

When the house is finished, the pigs make Mr Wolf a giant cup of hot chocolate with extra marshmallows.

"A good superhero should **always** have a reward,"

says the littlest pig. Mr Wolf loves hot chocolate!

What's the time, Mr Wolf?
It's **5** o'clock.

It's dinner time and the three little pigs have come round to Mr Wolf's house for a delicious feast!

Munch!

"It's hungry work, being a superhero. **Yum! Yum!**" says Mr Wolf.

Slurp!

What's the time, Mr Wolf?

It's 6 o'clock.

Mr Wolf has had a wonderful day of being a superhero and now he is feeling quite tired.

What's the Time Mr Wolf?

He tucks himself into bed with a special bedtime story.

"A superhero **always** needs a good night's sleep," he says with a big yawn.